E   Schweninger, Ann
       Valentine friends. Viking, 1988.

Ann Schweninger

Valentine Friends

Buttercup   Lucy

Viking Kestrel

VIKING KESTREL
Viking Penguin Inc., 40 West 23rd Street, New York, New York 10010, U.S.A.
Penguin Books Ltd, 27 Wrights Lane, London W8 5TZ (Publishing & Editorial) and
Harmondsworth, Middlesex, England (Distribution & Warehouse)
Penguin Books Australia Ltd, Ringwood, Victoria, Australia
Penguin Books Canada Limited, 2801 John Street, Markham, Ontario, Canada L3R 1B4
Penguin Books (N.Z.) Ltd, 182–190 Wairau Road, Auckland 10, New Zealand

Copyright © Ann Schweninger, 1988
All rights reserved
First published in 1988 by Viking Penguin Inc.
Published simultaneously in Canada
Printed in Japan by Dai Nippon Printing Co. Ltd.
Set in Windsor Light
1   2   3   4   5   92   91   90   89   88

Library of Congress Cataloging-in-Publication Data
Schweninger, Ann.   Valentine friends/by Ann Schweninger.
p.   cm.
Summary: The Rabbit family's Valentine's Day party is filled with
fun and surprises for everyone, including some special surprise valentines
that show two best friends just how special Valentine's Day can be.
ISBN 0-670-81448-2
[1. Valentine's Day—Fiction.   2. Rabbits—Fiction.
3. Friendship—Fiction.]   I. Title.
PZ7.S41263Val   1988   [E]—dc19   87-22326

Getting Ready

Perfect Hearts

Fold a piece
of paper in half
like this:

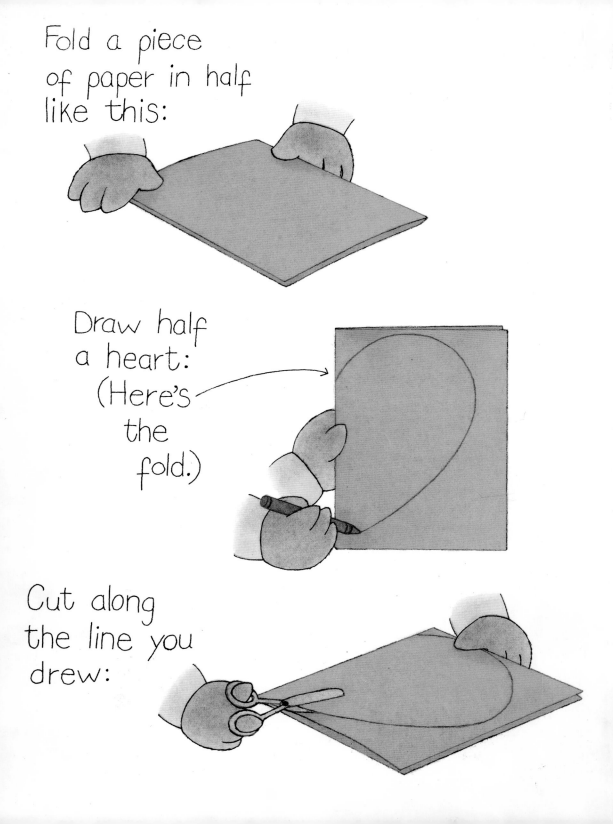

Draw half
a heart:
(Here's
    the
      fold.)

Cut along
the line you
drew:

Unfold the paper:

A perfect heart!

Special Delivery

Buttercup's daddy:

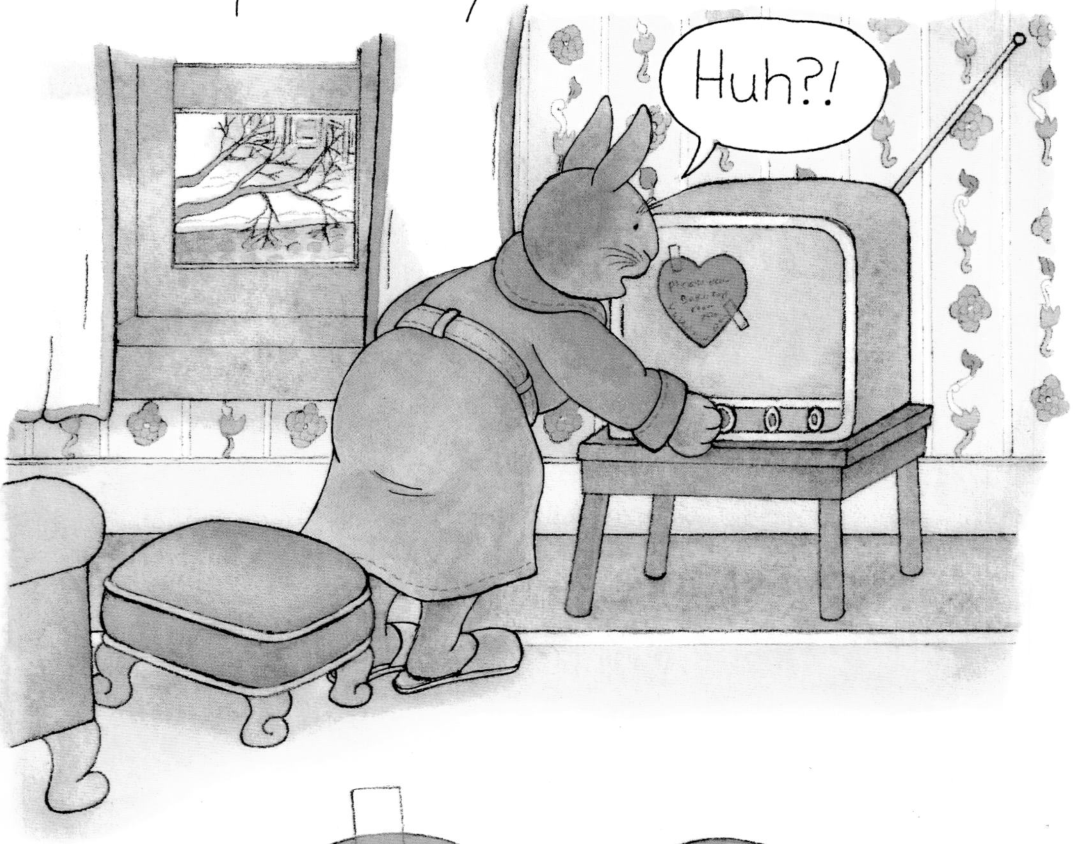

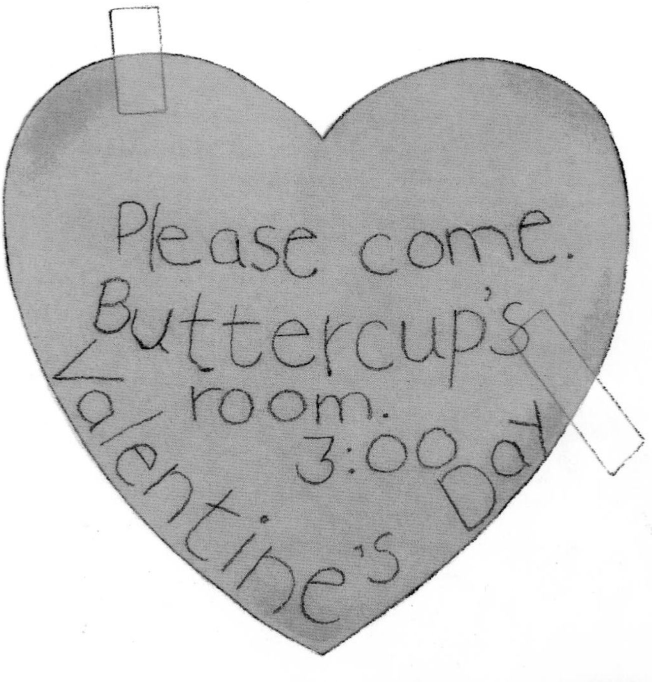

Lucy's dad:

Button Brown:

Making Valentines

Let's make valentines.

We have red paper

for making hearts.

Glue

and glitter

and doilies

and ribbon.

And old buttons

for decorations.

Here are the valentines
we made...

Valentine's Day, 3:00 P.M.

Happy Hearts

Good-bye, valentine friend.